First published in Great Britain in 2014 by Andersen Press Ltd.,
20 Vauxhall Bridge Road, London SW1V 2SA.
Published in Australia by Random House Australia Pty.,
Level 3, 100 Pacific Highway, North Sydney, NSW 2060.
Copyright © David McKee, 2014.
The rights of David McKee to be identified as the author and
illustrator of this work have been asserted by him in accordance
with the Copyright, Designs and Patents Act, 1988.
All rights reserved.
Colour separated in Switzerland by Photolitho AG, Zürich.
Printed and bound in Malaysia by Tien Wah Press.

10   9   8   7   6   5   4   3   2   1

British Library Cataloguing in Publication Data available.

ISBN 978 1 78344 053 5

ELMER
and the
MONSTER

David McKee

Andersen Press

Elmer, the patchwork elephant, had just started
his morning walk when he heard a terrible roar.
"Look out, Elmer," the birds and small creatures
called out as they came hurrying past him. "There's
a monster!"
"A monster?" thought Elmer. "*Really?*"
He continued his walk.

A little while later there was another roar. "Don't go that way, Elmer," said the monkeys, swinging through the trees. "There's a monster!"
Then they were gone.
"A monster again," said Elmer. "Very interesting."

Before long there was a third roar.
"Was that you roaring, Tiger?" asked Elmer
as Tiger raced towards him.

"Certainly not, that was a monster!" said Tiger, and he disappeared into the jungle.

"Fascinating," murmured Elmer, and he went on his way.

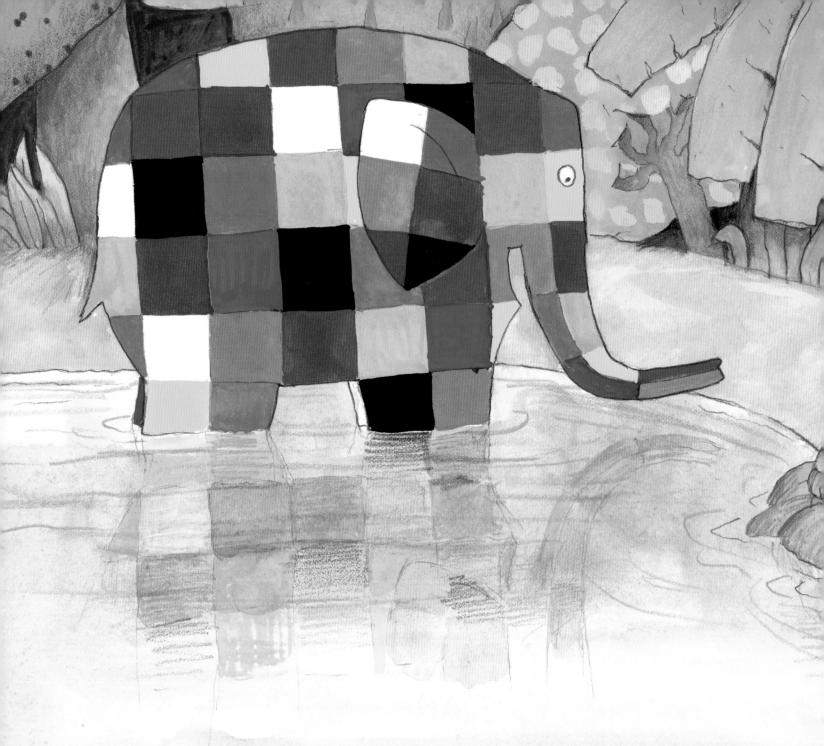

When the next roar came, Elmer was ready for it.
"Was that a monster?" Elmer called out to the crocodiles
as they fled past.
"Yes, a pretty monstrous one by the sound of it," said the
crocodiles. "Turn back, Elmer!"
"Or go on carefully," said Elmer to himself.

Soon after that there was another huge roar and Lion
ran by.

"Nice roar, Lion," said Elmer.

"It wasn't me," said Lion. "That's the roar of
a decent sized monster. I'm off to see where
everyone's gone," he explained as he ran off.

Almost at once another roar split the air. "Come with us, Elmer," called the elephants as they stampeded past. "There's a monster!"

"I have never seen a monster," said Elmer.
"You don't have to *see* it. Just imagining it is horrible
enough," said an elephant as he vanished after the others.

Elmer walked on. The next roar was very close. It shook the trees and sent leaves flying. Cautiously Elmer moved forward, ready to flee at any moment. He peeped through the trees and then pushed himself through into a clearing.

There, on a rock, sat a furry creature in tears.
"Hello," said Elmer. "Did you hear that roar?"
"That was me," sobbed the creature. "I do that when
I'm frightened."
"Why are you frightened?" asked Elmer.
"I'm just passing through on my way
home," sniffed the blue animal.
"But I keep hearing
monsters."

"Come with me," said Elmer. "I'll look after you."

Riding on Elmer's back, the furry creature chatted
happily until they reached the other animals.
"Hello, Elmer," said an elephant. "Thank goodness
you're safe. Who's your friend? Did you save him from
the monster?"
"This is Bloo-Bloo," said Elmer. "Go on, Bloo-Bloo,
show them."
Bloo-Bloo opened his mouth and . . .

ROAR!

The animals almost jumped out of their skins in shock. "Friendly, furry Bloo-Bloo is the monster you've been frightened of," said Elmer, laughing. "And these

friendly fellows, Bloo-Bloo, are the monsters *you* were
frightened of. You've all been rather silly, but it's
quite funny really."

So, laughing at their own silliness and sometimes whispering Boo! to each other, the animals happily accompanied the monster Bloo-Bloo on his way.